BLACK HOLES

Book for kids

Astronomy book for children

BY: BOOKSGEEK

BLACK HOLES
amazing space monsters

Have you ever looked up at the night sky and wondered what amazing things are out there?

Well, get ready for a cosmic adventure! This book will take you on a journey to explore one of the most mysterious and exciting objects in the universe: the black hole.

Ever wondered what a black hole is, how it's made, or if it could swallow up our planet? Don't worry, this book has all the answers! Let's dive in and discover the secrets of these amazing space monsters!

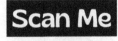

BY: BOOKSGEEK

BLACK HOLES
AMAZING SPACE MONSTERS

Welcome to the amazing world of black holes! Have you ever wondered what a black hole really is? Maybe you've asked yourself, "Can a black hole swallow everything?" or "Do black holes lead to other places like in the movies?"

Well, this book is here to answer all your curious questions! Together, we'll explore the mysteries of these strange and powerful objects in space. You'll discover how black holes are born, what happens if you get too close, and if they might even help us travel through time!

By the time you finish this book, you'll know all the amazing things they can do, and you'll see why scientists are so excited to learn more about them.

Get ready for an exciting journey to uncover the secrets of the universe's most mysterious and mind-blowing creations: black holes!

Before we begin Let me whisper a secret to you:

Before we begin, let me whisper a secret to you: Black holes might sound scary, but they're actually one of the coolest and most fascinating things in the universe!

TABLE OF CONTENTS

Black Holes
The Gravitational Pull

Imagine a giant, powerful giant vacuum cleaner high up in the sky! What a fascinating idea! If such a vacuum cleaner existed, it would have incredible suction power. It could pull all sorts of things towards it and it could be so powerful that not even light can escape it!!

What's So Special About a Black Hole?

A black hole is a mysterious place in space where gravity is super strong—so strong that it pulls everything nearby into it, even light! Scientists study black holes to learn more about the universe, but don't worry, even though black holes are super powerful, they're also very, very far away. It's like having a big, strong magnet in another city.

What kinds of things can black holes pull in?

Nothing can escape a black hole if it comes too close even light! This means it can suck in things like:

Space Debris

This means the remnants of old satellites, destroyed rockets, and other junk objects in space that are lost in space!

Asteroids
Think of asteroids as big rocks floating in space. They can be small like a house or big like a city!

Comets

Comets are like dirty snowballs made of ice and dust. When they get close to the sun, they heat up and leave a beautiful, glowing tail that can be seen from Earth

Planets

Planets are big round objects that orbit around stars . Our Earth is a plane

Stars

Stars are giant balls of glowing gas that light up the sky at night. Our sun is a star, and it gives us light and warmth.

Nebula

A nebula is a huge cloud of gas and dust in space. They can look very pretty and colorful.

Neutron stars

Neutron stars or (pulsars)are what's left after a very big star explodes. They are incredibly small and heavy, so much that a sugar-cube-sized piece of a neutron star would weigh about a billion tons!

INSIDE BLACK HOLES

Is a black hole really a hole?

Even though we call it a black hole, it's not really a hole in the way you might think of a hole in the space. A black hole is actually a very heavy object in space with a very strong pull. This means it can suck in things that comes too close even light!

NO, NOT REALLY A HOLE!

Do black holes really exist?

Yes, black holes really do exist! Scientists have found lots of evidence that black holes are out there in space. They use special telescopes and instruments to see the effects black holes have on things around them.

Even though they're tiny compared to the size of the original star, their gravity is super strong.

What is a black hole?

Imagine a black hole as a super heavy, dark spot in space. It's like a leftover piece of a star that used to shine brightly but, after many years, it "died" and turned into a black hole. Think about a fluffy marshmallow. If you could squeeze that marshmallow between your fingers, it would get smaller and denser. A star turns into a black hole in a similar way. When a very big star

What is Inside black holes?

Inside a black hole is one of the biggest mysteries in physics because we can't directly observe what's inside. We can not even see them! Scientists have some pretty wild guesses about what might be inside a black hole, but it's tough to know for sure because nothing can escape from one, not even information or light!

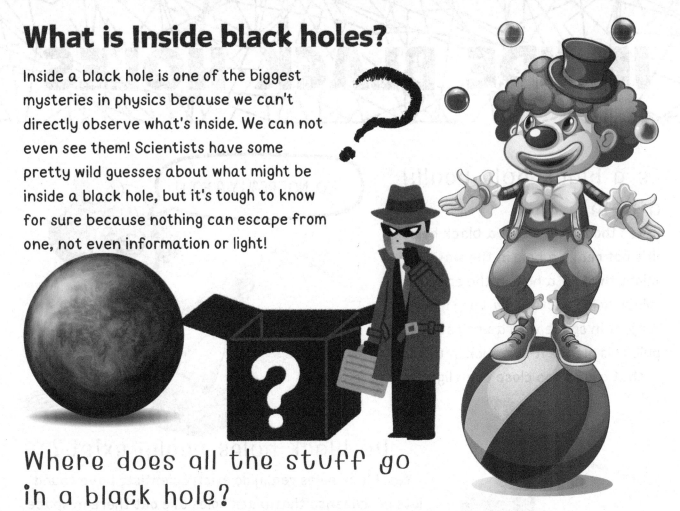

Where does all the stuff go in a black hole?

Most scientists think there's a point right in the center of a black hole where everything squishes into an incredibly tiny spot. This spot is called a singularity, and it's so squished that it's kind of like all the rules of space don't apply there anymore. Think of a big fruit which is huge and has lots of juicy parts. Now, imagine there's a tiny, tiny seed. This seed isn't just small, it's super dense—meaning it's really, really heavy for its size. Just like the seed is the core part of the fruit, the singularity is the core of a black hole.

Can we see a black hole with a telescope?

No light can escape from a black hole because its gravity is incredibly strong. Once anything gets too close, not even light can get out. This means we can't use a telescope to see black holes. It's like trying to spot a very dark black ball in a completely dark room—simply impossible to see. That why they are called "Black holes".

Travel to a **BLACK HOLE**

How do we know black holes exist if we can't see them?

Even though we can't see black holes directly because they're so dark, we can spot the effects they have on things around them. For example, if a star gets too close to a black hole, the black hole's strong gravity pulls on the star and can make it move differently or even tear it apart.

Why can't we visit black holes?

Visiting a black hole is impossible for now because they are very far away and dangerous.

Super Far Away

Black holes are incredibly far from Earth. Even the nearest ones are many thousands of light-years away. Traveling such a vast distance with our current technology would take far longer than a human lifetime.

Incredibly Dangerous

The gravity near a black hole is extremely strong. If we got too close, this gravity would pull on us so hard that it could tear apart anything, including spaceships!

TO BLACK HOLE

T-20

No Coming Back:

Once we get close enough to a black hole, there's a point called the 'event horizon.' If anything, even light, passes this point, it can't escape. So if a spaceship ever went past this point, it would never be able to come back out!

Light travels incredibly fast! Its speed is about 300,000 kilometers per second.

Mysterious Parts

What are the parts of the black holes? Black holes are fascinating objects in space, and even though they might seem simple because we can't see them, they are like space traps with three main parts! Let's imagine a black hole as a deep, dark well in space.

In a black hole, gravity is the boss, and nothing can escape its pull!

Event Horizon

This is the very edge of the black hole, like the rim of a well. It is the outer boundary of the black hole and the most important part. It's often called the "point of no return" because once anything crosses this boundary, it cannot escape the black hole's gravity, not even light. That's why we can't see inside a black hole; the event horizon traps everything.

Accretion Disk

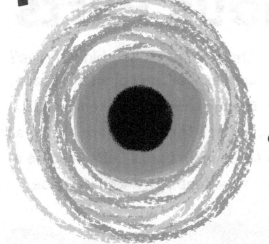

Around the black hole, there's a swirling, spinning disk made of gas and dust. It's like the water spiraling down the drain. The disk forms from material that has not yet crossed the event horizon, and it may or may not eventually fall into the black hole depending on many things. This disk glows because the material is moving super fast, rubbing together and getting really hot, emitting radiation that makes the disk glow brightly.. Accretion disks are amazing to observe.

Singularity

This is the very center of the black hole, where everything gets pulled into a tiny, tiny point. It's like the bottom of the well, where all the stuff that falls in ends up. the singularity is the core of a black hole, holding much of its mystery and secrets. It is incredibly heavy.

What is a Singularity?

Imagine you're drawing a dot with a pencil. That dot is very small, right? Now imagine if you could make that dot even smaller, so small that it's just a point with no size at all, but it's still incredibly heavy. That's kind of like what a singularity is. In a black hole, the singularity is thought to be the very center where all the black hole's mass is squished into a super tiny space — so tiny that it actually has no volume. That means it's just a point, but it contains a lot of mass.

EXPLORING THE EVENT HORIZON

This Magnetic Experiment" help you to understand the concept of the event horizon as the 'point of no return' around a black hole.

Place a strong magnet on a table. Bring a paper clip close to the magnet from the north until you feel the magnetic pull. Mark this spot on the paper as Point A. Repeat this process from other directions. You'll end up with four points (A, B, C, and D) around the magnet. Connect these points with a circle. This circle represents the boundary where you can feel the magnet's force, similar to the event horizon around a black hole.

The Event Horizon of a black hole is like an invisible area that surrounds the black hole in space. Once anything, like spaceships, satellites, stars, rocks, or even light, crosses this invisible line and goes inside the black hole, it can never come back out. It's like getting trapped!

Exactly, just as objects within a magnet's magnetic field are influenced by its force, anything that crosses the event horizon of a black hole will inevitably be pulled in by the black hole's intense gravitational force.

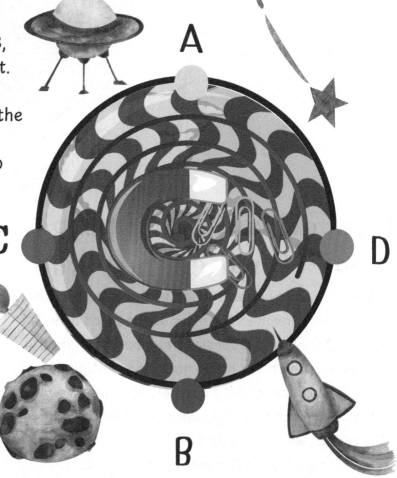

SCHWARZSCHILD RADIUS

Are all black holes the same size?

No, black holes are not all the same size. They can vary widely.

What is the Schwarzschild Radius?

The Event Horizon is like a magic circle around a black hole. If you cross that circle, you're trapped!
The radius of this circle is called the Schwarzschild Radius, which measures how large the black hole is.

Singularity

Event horizon

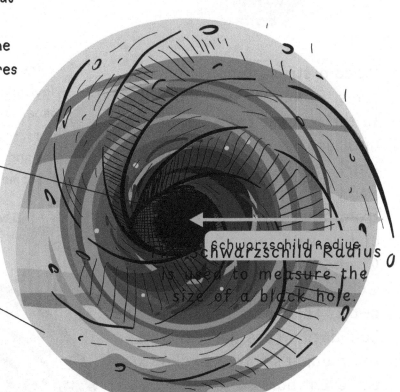

Schwarzschild Radius
Schwarzschild Radius is used to measure the size of a black hole.

How do we measure black holes if we cannot see them?

To measure the Schwarzschild Radius, scientists use a formula that involves the mass of the black hole, the speed of light, and a constant number from gravity. They take the black hole's mass and multiply it by two, then by the gravity number, and finally divide that by the speed of light squared. This gives them the radius, which tells them how small the black hole needs to be for light not to escape.

$$R = \frac{2GM}{c^2}$$

Where do black holes come from?

Many black holes in the universe were once stars. At the end of their lives, these stars collapsed into tiny black holes.

Many black holes were once big, bright stars! Just like a campfire that runs out of wood, these stars run out of fuel—fuel made from gases like hydrogen. When there's no more fuel, the fire can't keep burning. For a star, when it runs out of fuel, it can't shine anymore. The star then goes through some big changes.
There are lots and lots of stars in the universe, and they all look different. Some are big, some are small, some are hot, and some are cool. But when a really big star runs out of fuel, it can't hold itself up anymore and squishes down into a super tiny point that turns into a black hole.

But only the biggest and heaviest stars end up collapsing into black holes.

STAR TYPES

Do stars have different sizes?

Just like people, stars can be heavy or light, small or big. Some stars are tiny compared to our Sun, while others are absolutely gigantic! The biggest stars are called supergiants. They're so huge that if you replaced our Sun with one, it would swallow up all the planets out to Jupiter! On the other hand, there are stars much smaller than our Sun called red dwarfs.

Do stars have different colors?

Just like you can tell the temperature of a stove by its color (red is cooler, blue is hotter), we can tell the temperature of a star by its color.

- Blue and white stars are the hottest.
- Yellow stars like our Sun are in the middle.
- Orange and red stars are cooler.

Do all stars burn their fuel at the same rate?

No, stars do not all consume fuel at the same speed. A star that burns its fuel slowly will be cooler and redder. A star that burns its fuel quickly will be hotter and bluer just like candles.

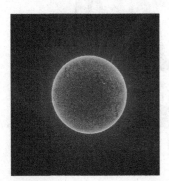

How are stars born?

Stars begin their lives in vast, cold clouds of gas and dust in space.

A star begins as huge clouds of gas and dust.

When gravity pulls these clouds together, they form a dense core known as a protostar.

A protostar keeps getting bigger by pulling in more gas and dust.

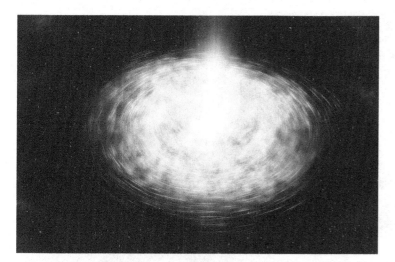

A star is born when nuclear fusion begins!

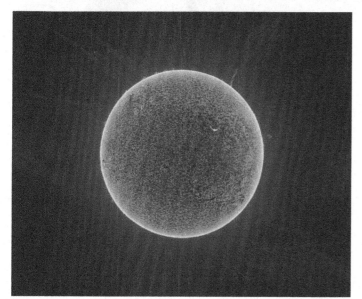

As more material is drawn in, the protostar grows hotter and denser. When the temperature and pressure are high enough, nuclear fusion starts, converting hydrogen into helium and releasing energy. This marks the birth of a new star, which shines by burning its hydrogen fuel.

The Stars' Core
What is the Star Core?

Each star has a special area at its center called the core, which is the hottest and densest part. It's the densest because it holds most of the star's matter and gases. You can think of the core as a crowded hall filled with gas atoms packed closely together. The pressure in the core is like the force you feel in a crowded room, where everyone is pushing against each other.

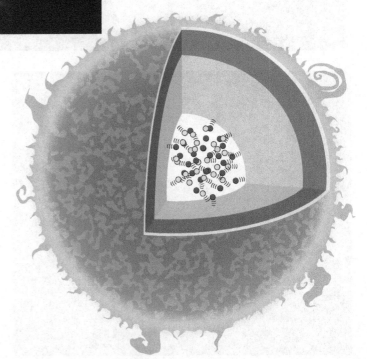

The center of each star is called the core.

Gases inside the star undergo incredibly high temperatures and pressure.

The core is the hottest part of the star, with temperatures reaching millions of degrees Celsius.

HYDROGEN & HELIUM:
The Stars' Fuel

What fuel do stars use to shine?

Imagine the stars in the sky as giant, glowing camp fire that need fuel to keep shining. The main fuel they use comes from two special gases: hydrogen and helium. Think of them as the magical gases that keep the stars burning and lighting up our night sky!

Hydrogen

This is the most common and the lightest gas in the universe. It's like the first building block of everything in space! Stars start their lives with a lot of hydrogen.

1
H
Hydrogen
1.0078

2
He
Helium
4.0026

Helium

Helium is created inside stars. As stars shine, they use up their hydrogen by turning it into helium. Helium is another gas, just a bit heavier than hydrogen. You might have seen helium in balloons that float up into the air when you let them go at parties. In stars, helium is made when hydrogen gases crashed and come together and join up under a lot of heat.

NUCLEAR FUSION

What is the Nuclear Fusion?

A nuclear reaction in a star is like a super powerful hot glue that sticks smaller things together to make bigger things, and when they stick, they burst out light and heat. In stars, it's mostly hydrogen particles sticking together to make helium, and this gives off a huge amount of energy, which is what makes stars shine. It's the same energy that powers the sun and gives us light and warmth on Earth. The core is mostly made up of hydrogen at the beginning of a star's life. During fusion, hydrogen atoms combine to form helium.

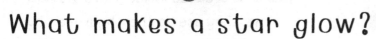

What makes a star glow?

Inside a star, hydrogen and helium are held tightly together by gravity. In the star's core, where it's extremely hot and compressed, hydrogen atoms fuse to form helium. This fusion process releases a vast amount of energy as light and heat, making the star shine brightly. This is the fundamental process powering stars like our sun.

How are stars born?

Everything around us is made from tiny particles called atoms. Imagine them as different colored beads that make up everything from the air to leaves to you and me. When these atoms come together, they form all the stuff around us.

He

Hydrogen gas found as double atoms connected together.

Helium gas found as single bigger atoms.

In Nuclear Fusion two or more small atoms of hydrogen, come together to create a bigger atom of helium.

Nuclear Fusion

BANG!

This reaction also produces a tiny, amazing particle called a neutron. It is very small but can lead to the formation of an entirely different type of star, which we'll discuss soon.

Neutron

Helium

He

STARS LIFE CYCLES

How does a star run out of fuel?

A star runs out of fuel after it has burned all its hydrogen, the main element it uses for energy. This process takes millions or even billions of years. As the hydrogen runs out, the star can't produce enough energy to keep shining.

Just like a campfire that runs out of wood, these stars run out of fuel over time. When there's no more fuel, the fire can't keep burning. For a star, when it runs out of fuel, it can't shine anymore. The star then goes through some big changes.

What happens when a star runs out of hydrogen?

When all the hydrogen is used up, the star starts to shrink. This makes the star very hot and squished together. The star then starts burning a different gas called helium. When it starts burning helium, it's like putting more and more air into the balloon. In this process, helium atoms crash into each other and stick together, forming heavier particles like carbon and oxygen. That cause the star to gets bigger and bigger. This is the start of the star's end. What happens next depends on how big the star is.

RED GIANT" PHASE

What is the red giant" phase

As stars exhaust their hydrogen, they begin to
fuse helium into heavier elements like carbon
and oxygen.

He

Helium gas found as
single big atoms.

When two **BIG** atoms of helium fuse,
they create a bigger atoms.

BANG!

Oxygen

He

He

O

Carbon

This process changes how energy is
produced and managed within the star,
causing its outer layers to expand.
The star grows larger and cooler,
often transforming into a red giant.
This expansion is a part of the star's
aging process, marking the beginning
of its approach to the end of its life.

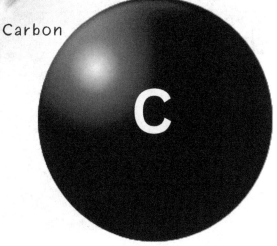

C

"WHITE DWARF" PHASE

What is the "white dwarf" phase?

After a star expands into a red giant, it eventually begins to shrink due to changes in its nuclear reactions. As the star runs out of helium to fuse, the core loses its heat source, causing it to collapse under its own gravity.

What forces keep a star from collapsing?

There are two main forces acting on a star:

Gravity Pull

Nucellar reaction Push

- **Gravity:** This force pulls all the star's material inward, trying to crush it into a smaller and smaller ball.

- **Pressure:** This force pushes outward from the star's core. It's caused by the heat and energy created by nuclear fusion, which is like tiny explosions happening inside the star.

These two forces are constantly battling each other. Normally, a star keeps its size because these two forces balance each other(equal) When they are balanced, the star is stable. But if one force becomes stronger than the other, the star can change dramatically.

How do stars die?

When the star run out of fuel it can't produce the energy needed to keep shining and to hold itself up against its own gravity. This leads to some dramatic changes, depending on the size of the star.

Why do Big stars die faster than small stars?

Think of it like this: A small car with a small gas tank can go a long way if it drives slowly. A big truck with a big gas tank might go faster, but it will run out of gas sooner. So, small, red dwarf stars burn their fuel very slowly, and they can live for trillions of years! On the other hand, big, blue giant stars burn their fuel very quickly, and they might only live for a few million years.

STARS LIFE ENDS

What happens when small to medium stars, like our Sun, die?

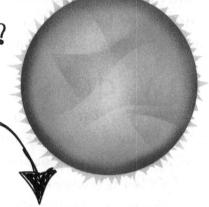

When the star run out of hydrogen it starts to burn helium after using up all its hydrogen

Then, the star expands into a

Red Giant

This is when the star swells up, becoming much bigger and redder.

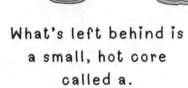

After that, the star sheds its outer layers into space, creating a beautiful glowing ring known as a

What's left behind is a small, hot core called a.

White Dwarf

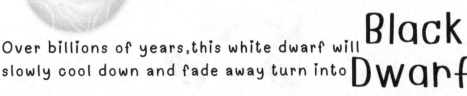

planetary nebula

Over billions of years, this white dwarf will slowly cool down and fade away turn into

Black Dwarf

What happens when Large Stars die?

The massive stars called blue giants.

The star's outer layers expand dramatically, and its surface temperature drops. This causes the star to appear red, hence becoming even bigger giants called

Red Supergiants

They are much larger than red giants and burn through their fuel much faster.

Eventually, the red supergiant explodes in a spectacular event called a

Supernova

which is one of the most powerful explosions in the universe.

What forms after the supernova depends on how heavy the core of the star is.

What makes supernova explosions so important?

When a star explodes as a supernova, it can become as bright as an entire galaxy for a short time. This makes them visible from incredibly far distances. Supernovae are responsible for creating many of the elements heavier than iron and spread them on the space. These elements are essential for life as we know it.

They also create Beautiful Nebulae

If the core of a star is very heavy, it turns into a **A neutron star**

If the core is even heavier, it can collapse completely into a

Black hole

a point in space with gravity so strong that nothing, not even light, can escape from it.

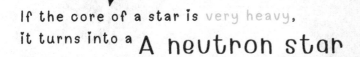

A neutron star is incredibly dense, meaning it's very heavy but small—imagine squeezing a huge mountain into a tiny pebble! It is made mostly of tiny, super-small particles called neutrons

NEUTRON STARS

Why Neutron stars are super special stars?

Neutron stars one of the densest forms of matter in the universe, second only to black holes.

They have super strong magnetic fields around them

A sugar-cube-sized amount of neutron star material would weigh about a billion tons on Earth!

Neutron stars spin around really fast.

When two neutron stars crash into each other, it's a huge event that even makes ripples in space!

They also give off a type of light we can't see, called radiation.

They send out beams like a lighthouse and that's why some neutron stars are called pulsars.

Why do some huge stars not explode?

Some really huge stars are so massive that when they run out of fuel, they don't explode like others. Instead they just collapse under their own extremely strong gravity.

What happens when these Very Massive Stars die?

They turn directly into black holes without a big supernova explosion.

How is a black hole formed from a star that doesn't explode different from one that does?

When a massive star collapses directly into a black hole without a supernova, it typically results in a larger black hole because more of the star's mass falls into it. In contrast, a star that goes through a supernova explosion loses some of its mass into space, resulting in a smaller black hole.

Types of Black holes

Does the size of a black hole depend on the size of the original star?

bigger stars make bigger black holes. Imagine a star is like a big ball of dough. If you start with a small ball, you'll end up with a small loaf of bread.

Are there different types of black holes?

Black holes vary in size depending on how much matter is compressed into them. There are four main types of black holes:

- Micro Black Holes
- Stellar Black Holes
- Intermediate Black Holes
- Supermassive Black Holes

How do the sizes of different types of black holes compare to each other?

You can compare the four types of black holes to sizes of a grain of sand, a rock , a mountain, and a dinosaur to understand their relative sizes:

If you imagine a supermassive black hole like a gigantic mountain!

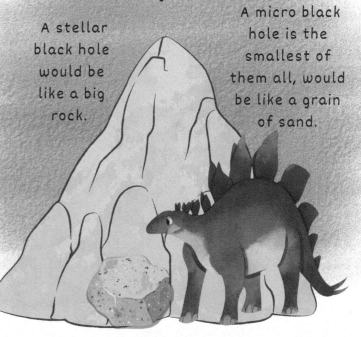

An intermediate black hole would be like a large dinosaur.

A stellar black hole would be like a big rock.

A micro black hole is the smallest of them all, would be like a grain of sand.

MICRO BLACK HOLES

What are micro black holes?

Extremely Small

Micro black holes are the smallest type and are theoretical. It means that scientists predicted them but they are aren't completely sure if micro black holes really exist. They're still trying to find proof.

Imagine a black hole so small you can't even see it with a microscope! That's a micro black hole.

They have other names like quantum black holes or mini black holes.

Extremely Hot

Scientists think these tiny space monsters might have been created right after the Big Bang. Unlike the giant black holes we hear about, micro black holes are super tiny.

They might even disappear on their own because of something called Hawking radiation. It's like they slowly shrink and poof! - they're gone.

Quickly Disappear

Well, if we find one, I'm naming it Tiny. Micro black holes? More like mini-mysteries!

micro black holes are thought to be the hottest type of black holes, if they exist.

So, while regular black holes are scary and huge, micro black holes are more like tiny, mysterious space particles.

STELLAR BLACK HOLES

What are Stellar black holes?

Stellar black holes are formed when massive stars collapse at the end of their life cycles. These black holes typically have a mass ranging from about 3 to 20 times that of our Sun.

X-ray emissions

They Help scientists to study and understand black holes evolution

supernova

They are created during supernova explosions when the core of the star collapses under its own gravity.

Stellar black holes have strong gravitational pulls, which can draw in nearby matter, forming an accretion disk that emits X-rays and other radiation.

Stellar black holes are like cosmic zombies. Once a star dies, it turns into one of these hungry monsters!

The first black hole ever discovered was Cygnus X-1 which is a Stellar black hole.

most common

They are the most common type of black holes found in the universe.

INTERMEDIATE BLACK HOLES

What are Intermediate black holes?

Intermediate black holes are like the Goldilocks of black holes - not too big, not too small. They're bigger than the ones formed from single stars (stellar black holes) but smaller than the supermassive ones found at the centers of galaxies.

intermediate size

Less common

Scientists are still trying to figure out exactly how they form. Some think they might be the building blocks for supermassive black holes, while others believe they could be the remnants of ancient star clusters.

Intermediate Mass Black Holes? More like 'missing link' black holes. We know they're out there, but finding them is like looking for a needle in a cosmic haystack.

IMBHs

Finding these intermediate black holes is tricky, and we haven't discovered many yet. But when we do, it will help us understand how black holes grow and evolve.

That's an IMBH. We're still trying to figure out if they're babies of supermassive black holes or something else entirely.

Imagine a black hole that's not too big, not too small - just right.

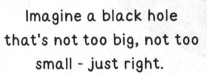

SUPERMASSIVE BLACK HOLES

What are Supermassive black holes?

Supermassive black holes are the largest type. These cosmic monsters are thought to exist at the center of most galaxies, including our own Milky Way. They are absolute giants of the universe. They're millions, or even billions, of times more massive than our Sun!

Giant monsters

At The Centers

Imagine a black hole so big it could swallow our entire solar system! That's how massive these things are. Scientists still aren't completely sure how they form, but they think they might grow by swallowing up stars, gas, and even other black holes.

Imagine a monster so hungry it could swallow YOUR entire solar system in one bite. That's a supermassive black hole for you!

(Sagittarius A*)

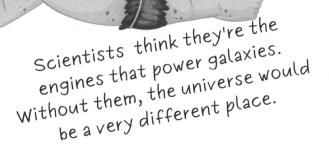

Scientists think they're the engines that power galaxies. Without them, the universe would be a very different place.

BLACK HOLES

Are you ready to embark on a cosmic adventure? Let's imagine a black hole in space with a powerful suction power that can pull objects towards it. Black holes are like cosmic vacuum cleaners, gobbling up nearby things. In this activity, we'll use our imagination and drawing skills to visualize 10 things getting sucked toward the black hole and flying around it. Let your creativity soar as you bring this cosmic scene to life.

BLACK HOLES

Imagine a colossal star reaching the end of its life and exploding. Choose your own colors to bring the supernova to life! Let your imagination guide you as you color the explosion. You can use vibrant shades like fiery reds, dazzling oranges, or even magical purples and blues. Fill the page with the energy and excitement of the supernova! At the center of the explosion, the singularity hides, a tiny point of extreme density and gravity. Now, use a black coloring pencil or crayon to carefully spot the singularity at the heart of the black hole.

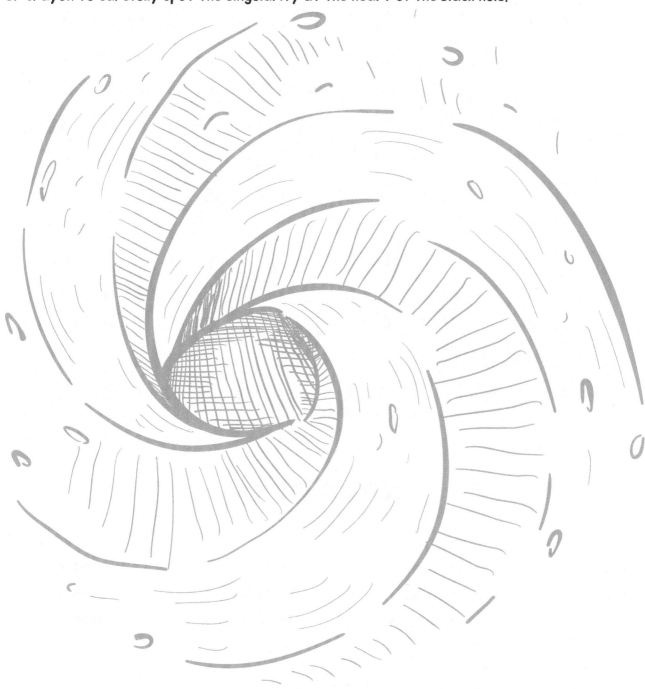

WORD SEARCH

```
M E Y B B Y N N V S T J R S Q
P T H Z Z F O E O I O R B I T
C D G L F H I U P N T S D D O
E L Y D S S T T M G A N O W R
T C O O U T A R U U C I W A G
J T I T P A L O I L A O F R R
A U G W E R L N L A L J W F A
M M Z O R W E U E R N F H S V
J T Q Y N A T K H I E B O Z I
D S G F O Q S O E T G U X V T
V K J O V L N X Z Y O K E P Y
E I K X A T O B D M R L E N A
R J F W N M C J L Z D N P C Q
O M O T N O I S U F Y F D F I
C R H I E R A H A U H K V H G
```

WORD BANK

- constellation
- dwarfs
- star
- core
- orbit
- gravity
- fusion
- helium
- hydrogen
- neutron
- singularity
- supernova

WORD SEARCH

```
C U J S N O I T A V R E S B O
B P H Y S I C S J K C F Z Q C
V F D L K D I S C I V W A C E
V Q E A I L G A L A X Y D G D
G P B N X X L A R Q T W F H I
S K X O S C C X S D E Q H C A
T F D I F I R A L L E T S C G
E O K T O M T H M B Q P U Y G
J R F A H S T T I H M V Y Y N
U M U T Y O N I E T S N I E C
P A G I S C L A C M N Z W Y P
I T G V A H A D Q B D X P S M
E I S A Y R E V O C S I D G Q
L O Z R S E V A W W U J T B P
V N N G Y H W O I W U Q Y W R
```

WORD BANK

- cosmic
- waves
- physics
- disc
- stellar
- galaxy
- jets
- discovery
- einstein
- formation
- gravitational
- observations

FAMOUS BLACK HOLES

What is (Sagittarius A*)?

Sagittarius A is a super-sized space monster living right in the middle of our galaxy! Imagine a giant, hungry space dragon sleeping at the center of a big, starry city. That's kind of like Sagittarius A*. It's so big and strong that even light can't escape it!

At The Centers

We can't see it directly, but scientists know it's there because they can see the stars and gas swirling around it. It's like watching water go down a drain, but in space!

Supermassive

Milky way

Sagittarius A* is like the king of our galaxy. It's a supermassive black hole, and it's calling all the shots! It's like the big boss living right in the center.

Don't worry about Sagittarius A, okay?* It's really far away and it's not coming to eat us or anything scary like that. It's just a big, sleepy space monster living a long way from here.

FAMOUS BLACK HOLES

powerful X-rays

Cygnus X-1? That's like the little brother of black holes.

What is Cygnus X-1 ?

Imagine scientists looking up at the sky and finding a super bright, mysterious light. They called it Cygnus X-1. After a lot of thinking and studying, they figured out that this bright light was actually coming from a super scary space monster - a black hole! It was like finding a hidden treasure chest full of space secrets. Discovering Cygnus X-1 helped scientists learn a lot more about black holes. Isn't that cool?

Small Black Hole

Cygnus X-1 is a smaller black hole, born from the death of a massive star. It's like a smaller, grumpy neighbor.
Cygnus X-1 is a famous black hole that was the first one scientists ever discovered. It's located in our Milky Way galaxy. Cygnus X-1 is special because it was found by looking at the powerful X-rays it gives off as it pulls in material from a nearby star.

Milky Way

Sure, it's scary and mysterious, but compared to its big cousin Sagittarius A*, it's practically a kitten.

This black hole helped scientists confirm that black holes really exist in space.

FAMOUS BLACK HOLES

It's a supermassive black hole that's putting on a cosmic light show for everyone to see.

What is M87 (Messier 87)* ?

Imagine a super-huge city filled with billions of stars. That's M87! It's a giant galaxy, much bigger than our Milky Way. And guess what? It has a super scary monster living right in its center: a supermassive black hole!

This black hole is so big and strong, it's shooting out a powerful beam of light and energy. It's like a cosmic laser show! Scientists took a picture of this black hole, and it's amazing! M87 is a really special place in the universe.

Super Massive

It emits the strongest X-ray sources seen from Earth.

First Photo

Hroom!

M87? That's the big kahuna of galaxies. It's got a black hole so massive, it's practically a cosmic bully.

M87* (Messier 87*) is a super famous black hole because it's the first one that scientists were able to take a picture of! The picture , show a glowing ring of light around a dark center, which is the black hole itself. This was a huge moment in space science!

FAMOUS BLACK HOLES

V404 Cygni? That's the space vampire! It's always hungry and stealing stuff from its roommate. What a drama queen!

What is V404 Cygni ?

V404 Cygni is a special kind of space monster. It's a black hole with a hungry problem! It lives with a normal star, kind of like a roommate. But this black hole is really greedy. It steals stuff from its roommate, like gas and dust.

When the black hole gets really hungry, it starts to eat a lot. It eats so much that it gets really bright and shines really strong. It's like a space firework!

stellar black hole

The black hole in V404 Cygni is about 9 times the mass of our Sun. That might sound big, but compared to supermassive black holes, it's actually quite small.

Scientists love to study V404 Cygni because it helps them understand how black holes behave when they're really hungry. It's like watching a real-life space drama!

"Swan" constellation

V404 Cygni is a black hole located in the constellation Cygnus, which is a group of stars shaped like a swan. This constellation is also known as the "Swan" constellation. Cygnus is found in the northern sky and is easy to spot because it contains a bright star called Deneb

GAIA BH1

The nearest black hole to Earth

What is the closer black hole to Earth?

The nearest known black hole to Earth is located in our Milky Way Galaxy it is called Gaia BH1. It's pretty far away, but it's the closest space monster to our planet! Scientists are studying it to learn more about these spooky space things.

What is Gaia BH1 ?

Gaia BH1 has captured the attention of astronomers worldwide. As one of the closest known black holes to Earth, it offers a unique opportunity to study these enigmatic cosmic objects in unprecedented detail. The discovery of Gaia BH1 helps scientists study black holes that are part of binary systems.

What is the binary systems?

A binary system is a system of two objects orbiting each other. These objects can be stars, planets, or even a star and a black hole, like in the case of Gaia BH1. Imagine two dancers gracefully moving around each other. That's kind of like a binary system. The two objects are constantly pulled towards each other by gravity, but their motion keeps them from colliding. This setup allows scientists to study how black holes and stars affect each other as they move together through space.

How long would it take to get to it?

Gaia BH1, which is about 1,560 light-years away from us. a light year is such a big unit of measurement.

Light moves really fast about 300,000 Meter per second

That's super far! That means light could circle around the Earth over 236 million times in one year

What is the lightyear?

A light year is how astronomers measure distance in space. It's the distance that light travels in one year. Since light moves really fast it can go really far in a year. Imagine running non-stop for a whole year; you'd go really far, right? Well, the light goes even further! In one year, light travels about 5.88 trillion miles. So , when we say the nearest black hole is 1,560 light-years to us that's an incredibly long distance,

> You tiny blue dot are so far away! I can barely see you. It's a pity I can't taste any of you. You're just too far away

Will Gaia BH1 swallow Earth?

No, don't worry! Gaia BH1 won't swallow the Earth. It's true that black holes are scary and powerful, but they need to be really close to something to pull it in. Gaia BH1 is very far away, so it can't reach us.

Think of it like a really strong magnet. It's strong, but if you're far away, it can't pull you in. Same with Gaia BH1!

NEWTON'S GRAVITY

WHO IS Isaac Newton?

Isaac Newton was a brilliant scientist who lived a long time ago. He discovered many things about how objects move and how gravity works. He thought that gravity is what makes things fall to the ground and keeps planets in their orbits around the Sun.

imagine the Earth is a giant magnet. It pulls everything towards it, like you, your toys, and even the moon! The stronger the magnet (or in this case, the bigger the object), the stronger the pull. So, gravity is like an invisible string connecting everything in the universe.

Why doesn't Newton's theory work with black holes?

Newton's idea of gravity as a pull between objects works really well for most things, like planets and apples falling from trees. But when it comes to black holes, things get more complicated. Newton's theory doesn't work with black holes because they have such strong gravity that even light, which has no mass, can't escape.

Newton didn't think about black holes.

This is where Einstein's theory of relativity comes in.

Every object in the universe, from tiny grains of sand to giant planets, attracts every other object. As the mass of either object increases, the gravitational force between them also increases..

Uh... apples fall down?

EINSTEIN'S GRAVITY

What is The General Relativity?

Relativity is a fancy word to explain Einstein's idea about the Gravity. Einstein has a mind-bending idea about how space, time, and gravity work together. He said that gravity isn't a force pulling things together, but it's actually like a curve in stretchy sheet!

The empty space isn't really empty!

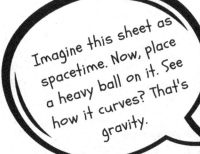

Look at this empty bag. It might seem like nothing is here, but according to Einstein it's actually full of something special called spacetime. Think of it as an invisible stretchy fabric..

Imagine this sheet as spacetime. Now, place a heavy ball on it. See how it curves? That's gravity.

What is the spacetime fabric?

Imagine empty space. You might think it's just nothing, right? But Einstein, a very smart scientist, thought differently.
He said that empty space isn't really empty! It's like a stretchy sheet. He called this sheet a spacetime fabric. Imagine the empty space as a giant trampoline stretchy fabric.

What is Einstein's idea about the Gravity?

Imagine you have a giant trampoline, and you place a heavy bowling ball in the middle. The trampoline bends under the weight of the ball, creating a 'dent' or curve in the surface. Now, imagine you put some marbles on the trampoline. The small marbles will roll or move toward the curve created by the heavy bowling ball. The trampoline's surface is no longer flat due to the ball's weight, so the marbles will be attracted toward the center of the dent. That similar to how Einstein explain Gravity.

According to Einstein, gravity is like how a heavy ball bending a rubber sheet makes a dent. That dent is similar to gravity pulling things toward the ball.

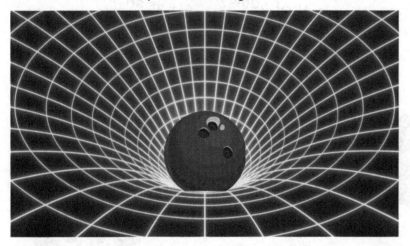

When something heavy, like a big bowling ball, is put on the trampoline, it makes a dent. Smaller balls that roll near the big ball will fall into the dent. This is kind of like how gravity works!

Big things like the Earth make a dent in space, and smaller things like us fall towards it.

Do all planets make the same size dent in space?

According to Einstein, no, not all planets make the same size dent in space. Imagine space as a big, stretchy sheet. Small planets, like Earth, make a small dent, while big planets, like Jupiter, make a much bigger dent. The bigger the planet, the deeper the dent it makes in space. This is why bigger planets have a stronger pull, or gravity.

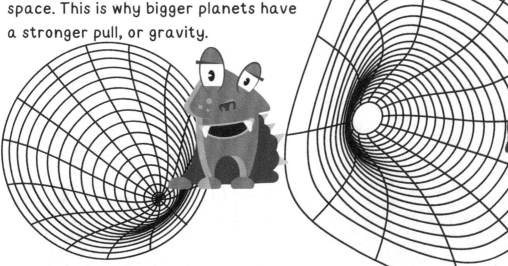

How does Einstein's theory explain black holes?

Imagine placing a super heavy bowling ball right in the middle. The trampoline would bend so much that it would create a deep hole. That's kind of like a black hole!

A black hole is a place where spacetime is curved so much that it becomes a bottomless pit. It's like the ultimate dent in the cosmic fabric. Anything that gets too close falls in and can't escape, not even light!

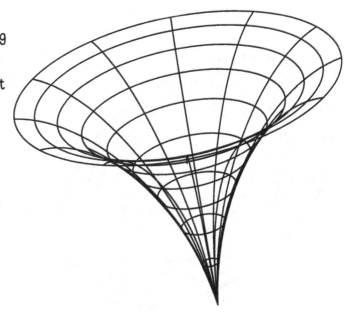

GENERAL RELATIVITY

young astronomers! Let's have a fun matching game! Here are three space celestial bodies with their respective masses:

1. Black Hole – Mass: 2,000,000,000,000,000,000,000,000,000,000,000 kg
2. Earth – Mass: 5,972,000,000,000,000,000,000,000 kg
3. Moon – Mass: 73,420,000,000,000,000,000,000 kg

Now, match each celestial body to the correct spacetime curvature around them.

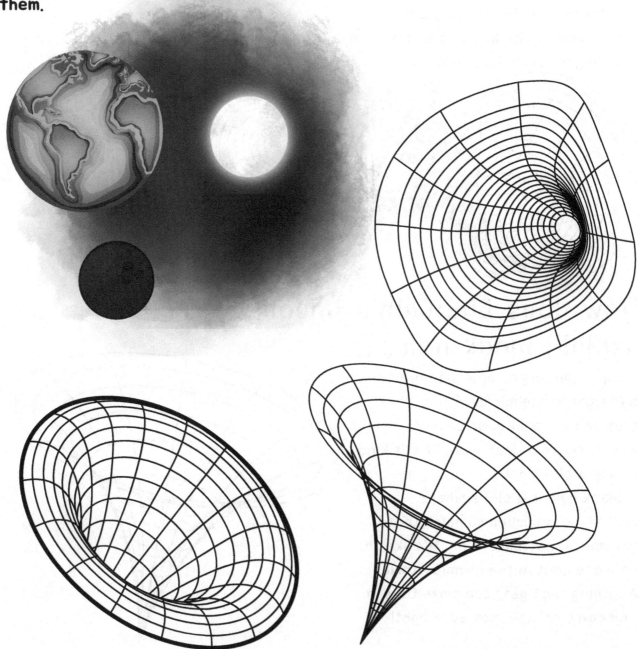

The singularity

Who was the first to predict the existence of black holes?

John Wheeler used the name (black hole) to describe these mysterious objects . They are completely invisible in space. They do not emit or reflect any light..

How is Einstein's theory related to the singularity?

The singularity is located at the very center of a black hole. According to Einstein's theory, a black hole is believed to have a singularity at its center. The math behind Einstein's theory predicts these singularities.

SURE!

Is the singularity actually possible?

scientists aren't sure if Singularities truly exist. This is because at these points, all the usual science rules start to break down and don't work anymore. Most scientists think that we need a new set of rules, which can really work well with the strange nature of black holes and make us understand what's going on in these extreme places.

Why do some scientists think the singularity cannot exist?

Some new ideas suggest that maybe there isn't a singularity at all inside black holes. Instead, there could be something like a quantum fuzz—think of it as a super squished, fuzzy ball where everything is mixed up but not squished into a single point.

Why are black holes so difficult to understand?

Usually, we can measure things like how heavy something is and how big it is. But at a singularity, all the matter being squashed into a point makes it impossible to measure by our normal methods. Imagine squashing an entire planet into something as tiny as a grain of sand. That's how incredibly dense a singularity is. It's like taking all the weight of a giant planet and concentrating it into an infinitely small point.

Because it's so incredibly small and dense, we can't measure it using our normal tools.

Imagine the deepest ocean trench you can think of. It's dark, mysterious, and goes incredibly deep. Now, imagine that this trench is infinitely deep and has no bottom. That's kind of like the dent a singularity makes in spacetime. It's not just a hole; it's a complete breakdown of our understanding of space and time. It's a place where our normal rules of physics no longer apply.

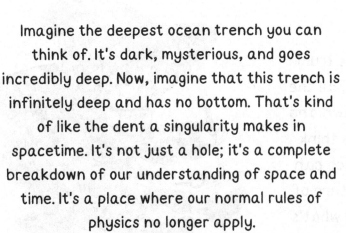

DEEP

STUDYING BLACK HOLES

Why do we need new science to understand black holes?

To truly understand them, we need a theory that can combine our understanding of gravity and realy big things (general relativity) with the rules of the very small things (quantum mechanics). This new theory, often called quantum gravity, is still a work in progress. It's like trying to fit a square peg into a round hole. We know the pieces of the puzzle, but we haven't figured out how to put them together yet.

STAY CURIOUS!

Why are scientists so interested in black holes?

Scientists are super curious about black holes because they're like giant cosmic puzzles! They want to understand how these space monsters work and what they can teach us about the universe. Plus, they're looking for clues about how the universe began and how it might end! Studying lack holes help us to improve our current understanding of physics, forcing us to develop new theories.

How do scientists study and observe black holes?

Studying black holes is like trying to capture a shadow. Since they don't emit any light, scientists have to be incredibly clever. They use different methods like Observing Nearby Stars and Gas, creating silhouette images and studying Gravitational Waves.

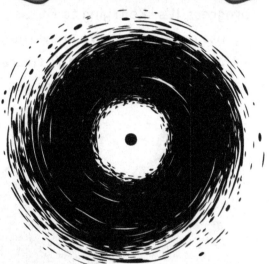

What does the silhouette of a black hole look like?

The silhouette of a black hole is the dark outline or shadow you can see when the black hole is observed against a brighter background, like light from surrounding gas.

The Shadow of a Black Hole

This dark area is where the black hole's intense gravity pulls in light, making it look like a dark spot in space. By using lots of telescopes from around the world together, scientists were able to take a picture of what a black hole looks like against a shiny background. This was a huge discovery!

Can Black Holes Collide?

Absolutely! Black holes can collide. Imagine two giant space monsters circling each other, getting closer and closer. Eventually, they crash together with a cosmic bang! That's basically what happens when black holes collide. When this happens, they create gravitational waves.

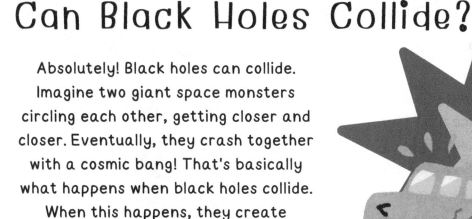

What are the Gravitational Waves?

Gravitational waves are like invisible ripples that spread across space when something really big and fast moves, such as black holes crashing and merging. Imagine tossing a rock into a pond and seeing the water ripple outward—that's similar to what gravitational waves do in space! These waves are tricky to see, but scientists use special tools to catch them, helping us understand more about black holes and the universe.

Are gravitational waves real?

Scientists have actually detected these waves, which is pretty amazing! The collision also creates a new, bigger black hole. It's like two super strong magnets smashing together to make one even stronger magnet!

Can Black Holes Move?

Just like any other object in space, black holes are affected by gravity. They can orbit around other objects, like stars or galaxies. Sometimes, they can even collide with other black holes! So, while they might seem like stationary monsters, they're actually part of the cosmic dance, moving and interacting with their surroundings.

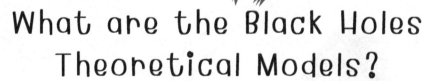

What are the Black Holes Theoretical Models?

Scientists use complex mathematical to understand the behavior of black. They create complex mathematical formulas to predict what black holes will do. Scientists then compare these predictions with actual observations to see if their models are accurate. This helps them learn more about the mysterious nature of black holes.

How do scientists learn about black holes by observing nearby stars?

If a star is orbiting an invisible object very quickly, there's a good chance it's a black hole. And when a star orbits a black hole, the black hole's strong gravity affects the star's motion.

By studying these changes in how the star moves, scientists can learn about the black hole's size, mass, and even its location. This helps them understand more about black holes even though they can't be seen directly.

How do scientists learn about black holes by observing X-rays and Gamma rays?

Black holes can heat up the material around them in the swirling disk called an accretion disk. to incredibly high temperatures, causing them to emit X-rays and other forms of radiation. Scientists use telescopes to detect this radiation.

Exploring Black Holes with Robotic Missions.

Did you know that we can't go visit black holes because they are really, really far away and super dangerous? But that's okay! We have amazing robots and cool spacecraft that can go explore for us! These awesome robots are like space detectives. They have special tools and sensors that let them get close to black holes, study them, and send back exciting information about their strong pull, the stars around them, and even whole galaxies!

One of our star space detectives is the James Webb Space Telescope. It's going to help us learn lots about how black holes start and how they help shape the universe.

Thanks to these robotic missions, we're on an exciting adventure to uncover the secrets of black holes and explore the wonders of space. Isn't that thrilling?4

James Webb Space Telescope is able to see what the universe looked like   back to 100 million years.

light travels super fast, and it takes time to reach us from faraway places in space. So when JWST observes distant galaxies and stars, the light it captures has been traveling for millions of years to reach us.

By studying this ancient light, scientists can learn about how the universe was long ago. They can see baby galaxies, early stars, and even catch glimpses of the Big Bang, which is like the universe's birthday!

What are the biggest challenges scientists face when studying black holes?

Invisibility: Black holes don't emit any light, making them incredibly difficult to observe directly. We can only study them by observing their effects on nearby matter.

Extreme Conditions: The environment around a black hole is incredibly harsh, with extreme gravity and temperatures. This makes it challenging to build instruments that can withstand such conditions.

MYSTERY

DANGER

CHALLENGE

BREAK THE RULES

Distance: Most black holes are extremely far away, making it difficult to gather enough data to study them in detail.

Our current science and math rules don't work well with mysterious objects like black holes, making it hard for us to fully understand them.

A COSMIC NOODLE EFFECT

What Happens If You Fall Into a Black Hole?

As you get closer to the black hole, the gravitational pull becomes incredibly strong. This force would stretch your body like spaghetti, a process called spaghettification. It's not a pretty sight! Once you cross the event horizon, the point of no return, you're doomed. You'd be pulled further and further into the black hole until you reached the singularity, a point of infinite density where our understanding of physics breaks down.

What is the spaghettification?

Spaghettification is a funny-sounding word for a scary thing that happens near a black hole. If something gets too close, the black hole's gravity pulls so strongly that it stretches the object out, making it look like a long piece of spaghetti. This happens because the gravity at the black hole's center is much stronger than at its edges, pulling the object apart. Imagine a person falling feet-first towards a black hole. The gravitational pull on their feet would be significantly stronger than the pull on their head. This difference in gravitational force, known as tidal force, would stretch the person out like a strand of spaghetti.

Can You Escape a Black Hole?

Once you cross the event horizon, the point of no return, there's no turning back. The gravity is so incredibly strong that nothing, not even light, can escape. It's like falling off a waterfall and trying to swim upstream - impossible!

Could a black hole swallow us?

Don't worry, a black hole isn't going to swallow us up anytime soon! While black holes have a super strong pull, they need to be really close to something to pull it in. The closest black hole to us is still very, very far away. It's like being afraid of a giant magnet on the other side of the world. It might be strong, but it's too far away to affect you!

Do black holes make sounds?

Sound needs a medium to travel through, like air or water. Space is almost a complete vacuum, so there's nothing for sound waves to travel through. However, there's a fascinating twist to this story. NASA has managed to sonify data from a black hole, turning the vibrations of the black hole into sound waves we can hear. It's not the actual sound of the black hole, but it's a way to visualize and hear the data collected about it

What Is a Quasar?

A quasar is an incredibly bright and distant object in space. Imagine a supermassive black hole at the center of a galaxy, gobbling up huge amounts of gas and dust. As this material falls into the black hole, it gets superheated and releases a tremendous amount of energy. This energy is what makes quasars shine so brightly.

How Do Black Holes Grow?

There are two main ways they do this

Accretion:

This is like a cosmic feeding frenzy. Black holes pull in gas, dust, and even stars from their surroundings. As this material spirals inward, it heats up and releases energy, often creating bright disks around the black hole.

Mergers:

Black holes can collide and merge with each other. This is a violent event that releases powerful gravitational waves and creates an even larger black hole.

How Do Black Holes Affect Light?

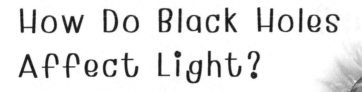

Black holes are like cosmic "light-eaters." When the light gets too close to a black hole, it can't escape the powerful pull, so the black hole swallows it up! Black holes have a big appetite for all kinds of light!

When a star gets too close to a black hole, its light can be absorbed and never escape. Black holes can also eat up infrared light, which is a type of light we can't see but can detect with special instruments. They can also consume gamma rays produced by other cosmic events.

That's why black holes are called "black" – they don't give off any light themselves and remain invisible to our eyes. They are like the dark ninjas of the universe!

Come close, light, vanish forever in my cosmic embrace.

What does gravitational lensing mean?

Picture a black hole in space as a supermassive ball with extreme gravity. When light from stars or galaxies passes near a black hole, its gravity acts like that magnifying lense, bending the light's path. This bending of light is called gravitational lensing. The black hole's gravity is so strong that it can bend and warp light from objects far behind it.

Scientists use telescopes to observe this fascinating effect. They look for stars or galaxies that appear in unusual places because of the black hole's gravitational lensing.

Related theories

What's the difference between black holes and wormholes?

Wormholes are theoretical tunnels through spacetime that could potentially connect two different points in the universe or even different universes. Imagine a shortcut through space! While black holes are a proven reality, wormholes are still just a theoretical concept. Scientists aren't sure if they actually exist. Some theories suggest that a special kind of wormhole might connect the insides of two black holes, but this is still purely theoretical.

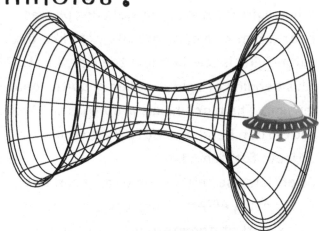

What Are White Holes?

Imagine a black hole as a cosmic vacuum cleaner, sucking everything in. A white hole is like a cosmic firehose, spewing out matter and energy.

They are regions of spacetime where matter and energy can escape, but nothing can enter. However, it's important to note that white holes are purely imaginary objects. No one has ever observed a white hole, and many scientists doubt their existence. They are more of a mathematical concept that arises from the equations of general relativity.

How Do Black Holes Affect Time?

Black holes have a strange effect on time: they slow it down. This is called time dilation.

Why does this happen? It's because black holes have incredibly strong gravity. This gravity warps the fabric of spacetime, making time move differently near them. So, if you were near a black hole, time would pass slower for you compared to someone far away. It's like living in slow motion!

Imagine two aliens, both of the same age. One stays on Mars, and the other goes on a cosmic adventure near a black hole. When the alien near the black hole comes back to Mars, his clock will show a different time than his friend's clock on Mars. The alien who spent time near the black hole will have aged less than his friend on Mars!

SLOW DOWN

It's like a magical time-traveling experience! It's like the black hole creates a slow-motion effect on time! The closer the watch gets to the black hole, the more intense the gravitational pull, and this warps the fabric of spacetime, affecting how time behaves.

Can black holes be used for time travel?

While some theories suggest it might be possible to travel to the past through a black hole, it's incredibly complex and might not even be possible. Plus, even if it were, surviving the journey would be nearly impossible.

What is Hawking Radiation?

Hawking radiation is a very special thing that happens around black holes.

Imagine empty space is like a busy playground. Tiny particles are popping up and disappearing all the time. !

When this happens near a black hole, something strange can occur. One of these tiny particles might get pulled into the black hole, while the other one escapes. The particle that escapes is called Hawking radiation. It's like the black hole is slowly losing energy by letting out these tiny particles. This process is very slow, but over billions of years, it could cause a black hole to disappear completely

WORDS LIST

- Accretion Disk
- Albert Einstein
- Apparent Horizon
- Asteroids
- Astronomy
- Big Bang
- Binary System
- Black Dwarf
- Black Hole
- Collapse
- Collide
- Contraction
- Core
- Cosmic Horizon
- Cosmic Microwave
- Cosmic Rays
- Cosmic String
- Cosmos
- Curvature
- Cygnus X-1
- Dark Nebula
- Dark Star
- Density
- Electromagnetic Spectrum
- Elliptical Galaxy
- Energy
- Escape Velocity
- Event Horizon
- Explosion
- Force
- Fusion
- Galaxy
- Galaxy Cluster
- Gamma Ray
- Gas Cloud
- General Relativity
- Gravitational Waves
- Gravity
- Hawking Radiation
- Helium
- Horizon
- Intermediate
- Interstellar
- Invisible
- Jets
- Light
- Light-year
- Magnetar
- Magnetism
- Mass
- Matter
- M87
- Meteor
- Micro

- Milky Way
- Nebula
- Neutron
- Neutron Star
- Observation
- Orbit
- Oscillation
- Particle
- Plasma
- Prediction
- Proton
- Pull
- Pulsar
- Push
- Quanta
- Quantum
- Quantum Mechanics
- Quasar
- Radiation
- Radio Waves
- Red Dwarf
- Red Giant
- Relativity
- Rotation
- Sagittarius A*
- Satellite
- Schwarzschild Radius
- Simulation
- Singularity
- Solar System
- Space
- Space-time
- Spaghettification
- Spin
- Star
- Star Cluster
- Star Formation
- Supermassive
- Supernova
- Telescope
- Theory
- Time Dilation
- Tidal Force
- Ultraviolet
- Universe
- V404 Cygni
- White Dwarf
- WIMPs
- Wormhole
- X-ray

Made in the USA
Coppell, TX
11 December 2024